D0876246

GAVIN MCNALLY'S YEAR OFF

HUNTING THE TREASURE

by Emma Bland Smith
illustrated by Mirelle Ortega

Spellbound

An Imprint of Magic Wagon
abdobooks.com

TO EVERETT -EBS

FOR MY MOM, DAD, AUNT AND BROTHER. -MO

abdobooks.com

Published by Magic Wagon, a division of ABDO, PO Box 398166, Minneapolis, Minnesota 55439. Copyright © 2020 by Abdo Consulting Group, Inc. International copyrights reserved in all countries. No part of this book may be reproduced in any form without written permission from the publisher. Spellbound™ is a trademark and logo of Magic Wagon.

Printed in the United States of America, North Mankato, Minnesota.
052019
092019

 THIS BOOK CONTAINS
RECYCLED MATERIALS

Written by Emma Bland Smith
Illustrated by Mirelle Ortega
Edited by Tamara L. Britton
Art Directed by Candice Keimig

Library of Congress Control Number: 2018965020

Publisher's Cataloging-in-Publication Data

Names: Smith, Emma Bland, author. I Ortega, Mirelle, illustrator.
Title: Hunting the treasure / by Emma Bland Smith; illustrated by Mirelle Ortega.
Description: Minneapolis, Minnesota : Magic Wagon, 2020. I Series: Gavin McNally's year off; book 4
Summary: Gavin and his family are visiting Michigan's Mackinac Island. Gavin and his brother, Gus, take a nature walk. Gus goes missing! Gavin is annoyed as he searches for Gus. Will he realize he is still hunting for treasure?
Identifiers: ISBN 9781532135095 (lib. bdg.) I ISBN 9781532135699 (ebook) I ISBN 9781532135996 (Read-to-Me ebook)
Subjects: LCSH: Family vacations--Juvenile fiction. I Recreational vehicle living--Juvenile fiction. I Missing persons--Juvenile fiction. I Rescue work--Juvenile fiction. I Treasure hunt (Game)--Juvenile fiction.
Classification: DDC [Fic]--dc23

TABLE OF
CONTENTS

CHAPTER 1
ON THE FERRY

Leaning on the ferry railing, Gavin WATCHED Mackinac Island grow closer. This was the last BIG stop on his family's yearlong road trip. Tomorrow, they were headed home to Northern California. Gavin sighed. He wasn't sure how he felt about that.

"There are **NO** cars on Mackinac," his dad was telling his *little* brother, Gus. "People get around by horse and bike!"

"Can we go horseback riding?" begged his older sister, Chloe.

"Sure!" said Mom. "Anyone else want to go?"

Riding horses felt too cheerful right now. "I don't know," Gavin said.

"Can I do a nature walk in the state park?" asked Gus, STUDYING a map. "I want to find this flower called trillium."

"Gavin, maybe you could go with Gus," suggested Dad. "I have to do RESEARCH at the island's library."

Gavin nodded, *sighing*. Great. He'd be spending his final day babysitting.

Then, with a **GRIMACE**, he remembered that he still had one "Personal Project" to complete. *Seek treasure.* He'd been avoiding this one. What did it mean? Was he actually supposed to hunt for HIDDEN treasure?

Gavin FLIPPED through the guidebook. Hey, there was an old fort on the island! Maybe he could find, like, an antique musket. From the map, it looked like the TRAIL Gus wanted to take ended near the fort. Maybe this day wouldn't be so BAD after all!

The **clang** of the boat against the dock *jolted* Gavin back to reality. They'd arrived!

CHAPTER 2
NATURE WALK FAIL

Everyone **FILED** off the ferry.

"We're meeting back here at the dock at six," said Mom. "Got that, boys?"

Mom, Dad, and Chloe took off. Gavin and Gus *wandered* down the main street.

"WHOA," said Gavin. It looked like a movie set. Victorian storefronts lined the street. Horse-drawn carriages CLIP-CLOPPED past.

As they walked, Gavin told Gus his PLAN. "So we have to do the nature walk FAST, okay?" he finished.

"OK!" said Gus cheerfully. "Let's
go! The trail starts over here!"

An hour later, they'd hardly made any progress. Gus **STOPPED** every few feet to log flowers and trees in his notebook. At this rate, they'd **NEVER** make it to the fort!

Lost in thought, Gavin SUDDENLY realized he couldn't see Gus in front of him. He went around a bend. Still no Gus. Annoyance bubbled up.

Gus wasn't around the next turn, either. "Gus!" Gavin CALLED. He walked faster. The trail sloped STEEPLY and he looked over the edge. Did Gus fall down the hill? No, he would have yelled for help.

Gavin was *RUNNING* now.

The path opened into a clearing.

He STOPPED, panting.

Spanning a stone arch was a

BLACK metal gate.

Gold letters **proclaimed**,
"St. Ann's Cemetery."

CHAPTER 3
LOST AMONG THE GRAVES

Gavin took a step *BACK*. He didn't like cemeteries. No way was he going in. But then a *GUST* of wind blew, and with an eerie **creak**, the gate swung open.

Gavin *glimpsed* something yellow. Flowers! Gus probably went in there *looking* for plants.

Hesitating just a moment, Gavin STEPPED inside. He forced himself to walk toward the center. He turned in a circle, SCANNING the big cemetery. Trees blocked his view. Shadows made it hard to see.

Something moved and Gavin *JUMPED*! It was just a squirrel on a grave. He bent down on one knee to read the stone's old-fashioned writing. It was a kid's grave. A little boy.

Wind *WHISTLED* through the trees. Gavin shivered and stood up *FAST*. *Where* was Gus?

He walked to the far corner, then along the wall to the next corner. Nothing. He **TURNED** down a row. Had he already looked here? He shook his head, confused.

SUDDENLY, Gavin heard a different noise. He RACED toward the sound. Behind a tall, mossy headstone, his little brother was curled on the ground, crying.

"Gavin!" Gus *CRIED*, sitting up. "I got lost!"

Gavin hugged him. "Gus, don't ever run off alone again."

Then Gavin sighed. He was relieved to find Gus. But now there was no TIME to go to the fort.

Gus held something out to him. "*Look* what I found in the trillium," he said, wiping his eyes. "Maybe it can be your HIDDEN treasure."

Gavin stared glumly at the plastic coin.

"Thanks," he said. He didn't bother to explain to Gus that it was FAKE.

He **PULLED** Gus up.

"Come on, let's go. The ferry

leaves in an hour."

CHAPTER 4

ANOTHER MEANING

They *trudged* down the hill toward the dock.

On the ferry ride back, Gavin was silent. By the time they climbed into the RV, a light rain was FALLING.

Mom **TURNED** around.

"Do you guys have homework to finish?"

"I'm **DONE** with mine!" said Chloe.

I'm not, thought Gavin **glumly**.
He watched the forest FLASH
by. Had he really thought he'd find
treasure at that old fort in this
century?

Then, he *wondered*
aloud, "Does *treasure* have a
meaning I don't know about?"

Gus **PULLED** out his dictionary. "How about this? '*Treasure. Verb. To retain carefully. To cherish.*'"

Gavin thought. Then he wiggled something off the zipper of his backpack. A dog tag. "Daisy," he whispered. He set it on the table.

Next he **PULLED** a bookmark
out of his social studies textbook.
It was a brochure for a mountain
INN.

Chloe looked over. "That was a *fun* day," she said.

He smiled and put the brochure next to the dog tag.

Gavin *rummaged* in a backpack pocket for his alligator key chain, the one he'd bought at the swamp tour gift shop. He hoped those baby alligators were **FREE** now. He added the key chain to his collection.

"Don't *forget* this," said
Gus. He set the plastic coin next
to the dog tag, brochure, and key
chain.

Images of *searching* for Gus
in the cemetery flitted past Gavin's
EYES. "*Seek treasure*," he said.

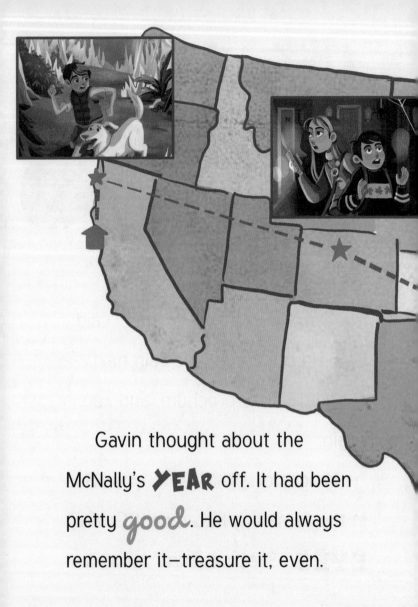

Gavin thought about the McNally's **YEAR** off. It had been pretty *good*. He would always remember it—treasure it, even.

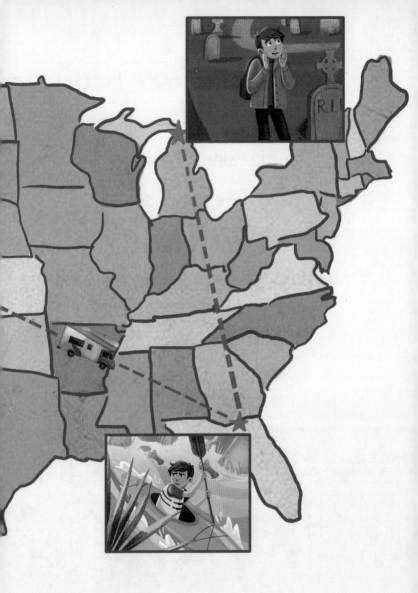

Gavin *leaned* back in his seat. Late-evening sun streamed through the rain. A rainbow STRETCHED over the sky. He'd had some amazing adventures. And now he was ready to go home.